MUSTANG - from Spanish:
"mesteno"
strays from the
mesta.
cattle raisers/mustangs
were horses that escaped from the mestas

2005

CHEYENNE MEDICINE HAT

Ten thousand years ago, the native wild horses of North America mysteriously disappeared. But in 1519, Spanish conquistador Hernan Cortes and his soldiers landed on the coast of Mexico with sixteen Spanish mounts, thereby reintroducing the horse to its ancient range.

In time, European settlers of a young America moved west, bringing with them heavy draft horses, Arabians, and other breeds that sometimes escaped or were set free when homesteads failed. Many of these animals survived to give birth to new wild bands. And the Plains Indians, at the height of their glory in the 1800s, even developed new breeds such as the Appaloosa. With vast prairies available, more than a hundred thousand of these "mustangs" (from the Spanish word *mesteno*, meaning mixed-blood) roamed over ten western states.

At the turn of the 20th century, sheep and cattle ranchers declared war on the wild horses, as the herds consumed range grasses needed to feed livestock. For decades, wild horses were exterminated. Tens of thousands were shot, poisoned, or driven over cliffs. Others were captured by mustangers for rodeo stock or sent to processing plants to end up as feed for poultry and pets.

Eventually, American public sentiment demanded an end to the slaughter. In 1971, the Wild Free-Roaming Horse and Burro Act was passed. Wild populations are now protected and monitored by the Bureau of Land Management, which sponsors a wild horse adoption program as a population control measure. Since 1973, more than 144,000 wild horses and burros have found homes with private individuals, while others continue to roam free on government sanctuaries.

To the spirit of the American mustang, inspired by the Black Hills Wild

Horse Sanctuary in Hot Springs, South Dakota—*B.H.*

This is for my mother…gone so long, but whose enthusiasm for horses

touches and inspires me still—*G.M.*

Text copyright © 2006 Brian Heinz

Paintings copyright © 2006 Gregory Manchess

Published in 2006 by Creative Editions

123 South Broad Street, Mankato, MN 56001 USA

Creative Editions is an imprint of The Creative Company

Designed by Rita Marshall

Edited by Aaron Frisch

Printed in Italy

Library of Congress Cataloging-in-Publication Data

Heinz, Brian J., 1946-

Cheyenne Medicine Hat / by Brian Heinz; illustrator, Gregory

Manchess. Summary: A wild mustang mare tries to protect

her band from capture and from a stalking cougar.

Includes author's note about the history of

North American wild horses.

ISBN-13: 978-1-56846-181-6

1. Mustang—Juvenile fiction. [1. Mustang—Fiction.

2. Wild horses—Fiction.

3. Horses—Fiction.] I. Manchess, Gregory, ill.

II. Title. PZ10.3.H31765Che 2006

[Fic]—dc22   2005544632

First edition

2 4 6 8 9 7 5 3 1

CHEYENNE MEDICINE HAT

Brian Heinz

PAINTINGS BY

Gregory Manchess

CREATIVE EDITIONS

The mustang mare shook off the attacks of biting flies and raised her head. A suspicious cloud of dust rose from a distant plateau, and the mare put her senses to work. Nostrils flared, testing the air for danger. Her sharp eyes studied the land, and her ears twitched forward. She looked to the buckskin stallion who stood nearby, alert but not alarmed. The dust soon settled and all her senses delivered the same message: nothing out of the ordinary. It was safe.

But it wasn't safe. They were being watched from afar.

Although the mare stood tall and strong, it was color that set her apart from the other horses in her band. She was white but for two remarkable exceptions. One was a striking black patch on her chest. The other was the odd headpiece of black hair that covered her ears and crown, then wrapped down and around each eye. She was a Medicine Hat mustang, so named a century earlier by Sioux warriors of the western plains who

SHE WAS A MEDICINE HAT MUSTANG, SO NAMED A CENTURY EARLIER BY SIOUX WARRIORS.

7

believed her markings were sacred shields to protect them in battle. But that was another time and the horse knew none of this. She knew only that she was the lead mare and that it was time for water.

Her black foal, born that spring, remained close at her side, grazing on the rich buffalo grass and blackroot that covered the high bluffs. Medicine Hat lowered her head, nickered softly, and nuzzled the cheek of her colt. He responded by brushing his neck against her chest. The colt was the youngest member of the mustang band, which numbered seven mares, four foals, and the stallion.

Far below the band, the Cheyenne River flowed like a shimmering snake, shallow and clear. Silvery clumps of sage and shards of yucca broke up a stretch of heat-dried grasses that ran to the bluffs fringed in twisted juniper and pine. Wildflowers splashed the land, and the air was laced with the songs of meadowlarks.

Medicine Hat led the band down the boulder-strewn hillsides to water, stopping occasionally to look about. The mustangs moved in single file, the stallion bringing up the rear. Medicine Hat kept

the band to open ground and away from the canyon walls. There, the mare knew, a great cat prowled among granite rimrocks, crevices, and shadowy folds of stone.

The mustangs had never seen the cougar, whose dun-colored fur made him as much a part of the canyon wall as the rock itself. But they had smelled him, had heard his high, sharp growl in the darkness, and had once come across the remains of a mule deer brought down by his great claws. Safety was on open ground, where a wiry mustang could explode into a gallop and vanish in the curtains of dust thrown up by flailing hooves.

It was the heart of summer, and the Cheyenne River was the mustangs' playground. After drinking her fill, Medicine Hat enjoyed a dust bath, rolling about in the powdery silt of the riverbank while the stallion stood watch in the shade of a broad cottonwood.

A GREAT CAT PROWLED AMONG GRANITE RIMROCKS, CREVICES, AND SHADOWY FOLDS OF STONE.

The other mares wallowed in mudholes, twist-
ing on their backs in brown slime until their hair
was caked with protection against biting flies. The
foals dashed back and forth between the mares,
splashing through pools and over wet sandbars,
tails blowing like feathered plumes, kicking up
heels and wheeling about.

A sudden snort from the stallion brought the
mares to their feet and sent the foals running to
their mothers. Medicine Hat sensed it, too, the
faint vibration in the earth that ran into her
hooves and up her legs. It was the rumble of
approaching horses.

Six mounted men, leaning low over their
saddles, broke into view from a bend upriver.
Mustangers! Clutching lariats and slapping their
horses' flanks, they thundered forward.

A SUDDEN SNORT FROM THE STALLION SENT THE FOALS RUNNING TO THEIR MOTHERS.

The stallion whistled sharply and planted himself between the mares and the approaching riders. Medicine Hat understood the command and went to work. She circled the band tightly together, turned from the threat, and burst into a run, her black colt at her side. She took the band back across the river to a rocky slope that led to high ground, only to meet an outrider charging downhill, hooting wildly and blocking their path.

Medicine Hat nudged her colt and turned the band again to run along the shore and escape downriver, but a second outrider sloshed through the shallows, waving his hat, and turned the band back to close the trap.

The stallion flattened his ears and reared as two lariats swept through the air, fell around his neck, and tightened. Panic set in and his eyes rolled white. A half-ton of fury, he struggled against the taut ropes and lashed out with powerful kicks from his hindquarters. Two mares whinnied in alarm and fell to the same fate. The wranglers forced them upriver toward a makeshift corral, while their confused foals followed silently, refusing to abandon their mothers.

Medicine Hat dodged back and forth, working to keep herself between her colt and her enemies. One mustanger eyed the handsome colt and whirled a coiled rope above his head. Desperately, Medicine Hat plunged ahead and slammed against both rider and horse, knocking them off balance. Her teeth closed on the soft flank, and the horse went down, pinning the rider to the ground. There was a brief opening in the circle of riders, and Medicine Hat led her colt through it. They raced across the river and into the mouth of Hell's Canyon, deep into the realm of the great cat.

When Medicine Hat, lathered up and breathing heavily, finally stopped and turned, only her black colt and four mares were still with her. She stared beyond them. They were alone. The band of twelve was now a band of six.

There were some welcome rain pools trapped in hollows on the canyon floor, and enough tufts of grass to fill hungry bellies. So the mustangs rested and waited, their shadows stretching as the sun set.

Night gathered around them, carrying a cool breeze. The canyon walls glowed with moonlight, illuminating ancient Indian petroglyphs. Men would not come in darkness, but the cougar was always a threat. With the remaining mares close by and her foal asleep at her feet, Medicine Hat kept vigil. All night she watched for a flicker of movement, a shift of shadow.

Dawn washed the land in pale light. Although no danger could be seen, the morning air carried the smell of men and the faint click of iron-shod hooves on stone. The mustangers were on the move.

Medicine Hat whinnied, and the horses galloped deeper into the canyon toward a steep trail of loose rock that led up and out. To follow the trail, the band had to pass between two huge shoulders of stone where the canyon walls narrowed. Although Medicine Hat was fearful of such tight quarters, she knew freedom was on the high ground.

As the horses approached from upwind, the cougar crouched on a sandstone ledge, his eyes locked on the colt. His muscles tensed, and a twitch of his tail gave him away. The cat sprang, but Medicine Hat bumped her foal aside to shield him with her body.

The snarling cat dropped with claws extended and fell upon Medicine Hat's rump just short of his mark. He slid backward, tearing bloody lines in the mare's hip. With a scream, she kicked, twisted, and crowhopped to shake him off. There was a sudden thump of hoof against flesh, and the big cat rolled away and bolted. Riders had come into sight, and they were approaching fast.

⟨⟩

THE CANYON WALLS GLOWED WITH MOONLIGHT, ILLUMINATING ANCIENT INDIAN PETROGLYPHS.

Led by Medicine Hat, the mustangs raced for the trail on the canyon wall, a trail too steep for their mounted pursuers. Primitive spirit and hot blood surged through their well-muscled bodies as the mustangs struggled upward, sending loose rocks clattering down behind them. At last, they reached the high plateau, and freedom.

Over the next two months, Medicine Hat and her tiny band ranged farther west, to rolling lowlands of sweet grass where her colt could grow tall and strong. Autumn brought a north wind that swept the land and stained the cottonwoods yellow. It brought cool rain. And one day, it brought a lone visitor.

Medicine Hat watched warily as a painted horse appeared on the horizon and drew near. It was a young pinto stallion, dressed in broad patches of brown on white. As he kept his distance, pacing in a wide arc, Medicine Hat followed him with unblinking eyes. The stallion stopped. While the sun faded into clouds and reappeared, the two horses stood motionless, eyes fixed upon each other. The stallion took a few cautious steps forward and stopped again. Then, Medicine Hat nickered a greeting and ventured out to meet him.

MEDICINE HAT WATCHED WARILY AS A PAINTED HORSE APPEARED ON THE HORIZON.

Medicine Hat nickered a greeting and ventured out to meet him.

markings-
front patch
on Med
Hat chest

South
Dakota-
BLACK
HILLS

Institute
of Range & the
American Mustang

Cheyenne
Medicine
Hat

eye markings